DEPUTY
AT
WILDCARD

MARGARET SCARIANO

A **PERSPECTIVES** BOOK
Academic Therapy Publications
Novato, California

Cover Design and Illustrations: Herb Heidinger

International Standard Book Number: 0-87879-315-1

1 0 9 8 7 6 5 4
0 9 8 7 6 5 4 3 2

CONTENTS

CHAPTER 1

FIRST LOOK
AT WILD CARD

Lance Tyler was tired of sitting. He had been on the bus for eight hours. Then he saw a sign: Wild Card, Nevada — 20 miles. He was almost there. It would be good to see Aunt Charlotte. It would be good to breathe clean air. The smog in the city had been awful. Every day it seemed worse. He thought he couldn't stand another day. Then Aunt Charlotte's letter came. Wild Card needed a library, she wrote. Why didn't he visit her? Maybe he could talk the town council into opening a library. So here he was on a bus in the middle of nowhere. But at least the air was clean.

A half hour later the bus pulled into Wild Card. It was late afternoon. Lance stepped off the bus. He carried his duffel bag in one hand. In the other he carried his motorcycle helmet and goggles. He headed for the bus station. He would ask someone there how to find Aunt Charlotte.

1

Funny old Aunt Charlotte. She was the sheriff of Wild Card. Nothing that Aunt Charlotte did ever surprised Lance or his family.

At the bus station he asked the man where the town jail was.

The man didn't even look up. "Two blocks down the main street. Turn north at the vacant lot. You'll come to the blacksmith's shop. The jail is across the street." Then he looked at Lance. "But you won't find the sheriff there."

"I won't?" Lance asked.

"Nope. Ambulance came and took her off to Reno." The man scratched his chin. "Yep. About two hours ago."

"What happened?" Lance felt as if he'd been socked in the belly.

"Ask Jamie Parker," the man said. "He's the blacksmith. He was in jail. He saw the whole thing."

"What whole thing?" Lance asked.

"The sheriff broke her leg," the man answered. "It was the wet cement floors. She should never have skated on them."

"Aunt Charlotte was *skating*?" Lance asked.

"Roller skating, son. In the large room where the cells are. She was practicing for a roller derby in Reno."

Lance shook his head. He knew his Aunt Charlotte had always loved excitement. But roller skating at her age? For a roller derby? Good grief! What next? Two years ago she had sprained her back parachuting. Guess nothing should surprise him after that.

"Are you Charlotte's nephew from the city?" the man asked.

"Yes," Lance said. "Guess I better catch a bus to Reno. What hospital is Aunt Charlotte in?"

"You must be Lance. Charlotte told me a lot about you." The man reached under the counter. "She said to give you these." He handed Lance a silver star with "Deputy" printed on it and a ring of keys. "Charlotte said to make yourself at home. Her apartment is in the back end of the jail."

"What do I do with this?" Lance held out the silver star like it was a hot potato. "I'm a librarian, not a law man."

The man laughed. "Nothing to it. Jail is just like a library. Got to keep everybody quiet." He laughed again at his own joke. "Oh, yes, Charlotte said not to let Jamie out until Thursday. His seven days will be up then. And the other fellow. Now he's a bad one. Roy Clelland's his name. An officer from California will pick

3

him up on Saturday. Take him back there to stand trial."

"Is he dangerous?" Lance tried to keep his voice steady. It shook just like his knees.

"Lance, take my word for it. That Roy Clelland is dangerous. He was born mean," the man said.

"What do I do with this? I'm a librarian, not a law man."

"Well, thanks for the advice . . . and the star. I'll head up to the jail. Maybe I'll call Aunt Charlotte at the hospital." Lance picked up his gear.

"Oh, I almost forgot. A trucker was in this morning. Said he had a motorcycle for you. I told him to leave it at the jail."

"Thanks a lot," Lance said. He walked out the door and headed down the main street. The silver badge felt heavy in his pocket. What a bummer! Deputy! He hated guns. He didn't even like hunting. As for fishing, fish belonged in the water, not on a hook. Well, he'd do his best for Aunt Charlotte.

CHAPTER 2

DEPUTY OR COOK?

Lance passed the vacant lot. Ahead was the blacksmith's shop. Next to the shop was a small corral. Several horses stood in it. The big double doors to the blacksmith shop were padlocked. A sign hung on the building. It read: Horses for Rent and Expert Smithy. Underneath the painted sign was another one. It read: Closed for Vacation. Lance laughed. The man at the bus station had said the blacksmith was in jail for seven days. Some vacation.

Then Lance saw the building across the street. He knew it was the jail. There were bars on all the windows. He crossed the road. Aunt Charlotte's station wagon was in the driveway. It had 'SHERIFF' printed on its front doors. Then he saw his motorcycle. It leaned against the building. He'd have to find a safe place to keep it.

He walked up the steps into a small hall. There was a bench along the wall and some magazines on a table. Lance opened the hall door and stepped into a large room. On one side of the room was a desk, chair, and a file cabinet. WANTED posters were stuck on a bulletin board on the wall. Handcuffs hung from a wooden peg. A pearl-handled gun and holster hung from another peg. Lance shuddered. Aunt Charlotte might be able to shoot a wart off a snake's nose. But not him. He looked around the room. It was plenty big for roller skating. And big enough for his motorcycle, too. After he got unpacked, he'd bring it in. What could be safer than a jail?

Then he saw the three cells along the far wall. He walked across the room. There was no one in the first cell. He looked into the next cell. A small man with lots of white hair stood close to the bars. When he saw Lance, he grinned. Good grief! He didn't have a tooth in his mouth.

"Welcome, son," the man called out. "I'm Jamie. You must be Charlotte's nephew. She told me all about you. She's sure proud of you." He stuck his hand through the bars. Lance shook it.

In the next cell a man sat on his cot. He wore a black cowboy hat and a white t-shirt with the sleeves cut off. His jeans fit tight, and his boots were black, too. The man stood up and walked to the bars.

"Well, well. What do we have here? Some smart city dude?" A toothpick dangled from the man's mouth.

Lance hoped his pounding heart didn't show through his shirt. The bus station man was right. This man looked mean. His eyes were a cold blue. His mouth was thin and hard-looking. A scar ran from the tip of his eyebrow to the top of his ear.

Lance took a deep breath. "Hello. I'm Lance Tyler, your friendly deputy."

"There aren't any friendly deputies. I'm Roy Clelland. You probably heard of me. I'm *wanted* in three states." The man looked in the small mirror over the sink. He took off his hat and smoothed the sides of his head. Then he put his hat back on. He turned to Lance. "Yep, wanted in three states by the law. And in all states by the ladies." He looked at himself in the mirror again and smiled.

Criminy! This guy sure likes himself, Lance thought.

"Hey there. Has the cat got your tongue? I'm talking to you." Clelland stuck his face close up to the bars. "You aren't so darn smart you can't talk

8

talk to me."

Lance grinned. "Well, at least I'm smart enough to be on the outside of those bars."

Lance heard Jamie's laughter from the next cell.

"He got you that time, didn't he, Clelland?" Jamie said. "This here is Sheriff Charlotte's nephew. He's a librarian from the city."

"Shut up, you little squirt," Clelland said. "Is that right, Deputy? You a librarian?"

"Yes, I am," Lance answered. "I'm just here to help my aunt out for a few days."

"Got any books with you?" Clelland asked.

"As a matter of fact, I do."

"Sure would like to have something to read." Now Clelland's voice was low. "I read a lot. Not much else to do in jail."

"I'll see what I can find, Mr. Clelland," Lance said. He headed toward a door marked "private." He was sure that must be Aunt Charlotte's apartment.

Aunt Charlotte's apartment was comfortable. The living room had a large soft chair and a television set. There was a couch with extra pillows. Off the living room were two bedrooms. Lance could tell which was the guest room. It was very neat.

Lance emptied his duffel bag and put his clothes in the drawers. Then he went to the kitchen to get something to eat. He opened the cupboards. He had never seen so many cans. Cans of pork and beans, cans of stew, cans of spaghetti. There were hot dogs and eggs in the refrigerator.

Then he heard a clanging sound. It was regular and loud like the beat of a drum. It was coming from the large room with the three cells.

He opened the door and looked in. Roy Clelland was banging his tin cup against the iron bars. "What's wrong, Mr. Clelland?" Lance asked.

Clelland stopped banging the cup. "Where's the grub?" he asked.

"Grub?" Lance shrugged his shoulders. "I don't know anything about grub."

"Food, man!" Clelland yelled.

In the next cell, Jamie spoke up. "Lance, Charlotte is not only the sheriff. She's also the cook. She feeds us prisoners."

Now Lance knew why Aunt Charlotte had so much canned food. "I didn't know she cooked for you. I'll get right to it," he said.

Lance went back into the kitchen. He found a couple of trays. He reached for the can of stew. Then he put it back. He couldn't eat it. How could he expect Jamie and Mr. Clelland to? Then he decided to make up his own recipe. He put some beef hash in a pan. When it was hot, he dropped a poached egg on top of it. With some canned pears and beans the plate looked pretty good. He filled a mug with coffee. After the tray was loaded, he carried the first one to Jamie.

Lance set the tray down in front of the cell. He started to open the cell door.

"No, no, son. Don't unlock the cell. I might escape," Jamie laughed. "Put the tray on the floor and slide it under the cell door. Plenty of room."

Lance did as he was told. Jamie leaned close to the bars and whispered, "Be careful of Clelland. He's a bad dude. Full of tricks. And leave the cell keys in the kitchen."

Lance went into the kitchen. He unhooked the ring of keys from his belt. He laid it on the table. Then he picked up Clelland's tray. When he knelt down to slide it under the cell door, Clelland reached through the bars and grabbed his wrist. Twisting it, he said, "Give me your gun, Deputy. I'm not staying for supper."

CHAPTER 3

WANTED: A LIBRARY
IN WILD CARD

Lance groaned with pain. He said, "I don't have a gun. It's hanging on the wall over there."

Clelland twisted the wrist harder. "Your keys, then, Deputy," he growled.

"I don't have the cell keys either." Lance stretched his body so that Clelland could see his empty belt loop. "See. No keys. I left them in the kitchen."

Clelland swore. "You're the dumbest deputy I ever seen. No gun. No keys." He let go of Lance's wrist. He stood up. "It's guys like you that give the law a bad name."

Lance pushed the tray under the bars. He went back to the kitchen. That had been a close call!

That night he slept with the windows wide open. The fresh, cool air filled the room. There were no traffic noises. Lance heard a frog croak and the chirp of crickets. He pulled the blanket

12

around his shoulders. If he didn't have to be deputy, he would be very happy in Wild Card.

The next morning the ring of the telephone woke him. "Hello." Then he remembered. "Uh, sheriff's office."

It was Aunt Charlotte. Lance was glad to hear her voice. "When are you coming home, Aunt

Lance groaned with pain. "I don't have a gun. It's hanging on the wall over there."

Charlotte?"

"Just as soon as I get a walking cast," she said.

"I hope you get it soon, Aunt Charlotte," Lance said. Then he told her about Clelland trying to break out of jail.

"Lance, wear my gun. Act tough." Aunt Charlotte sounded worried.

"No way, Aunt Charlotte. Unless I'm willing to use it, I shouldn't wear a gun," Lance said.

"Lance, you're not in a library now. Clelland is dangerous."

"Don't worry, Aunt Charlotte. I won't let him get the best of me again."

Then Aunt Charlotte told him to see Mayor Dobbs. "He might help you start a library in Wild Card."

Lance promised to see the mayor that morning. He hung up the phone and went to the kitchen to make breakfast.

When he slid the tray under Jamie's cell door, Jamie looked him over. In a low voice he said, "Good. No gun. No keys. Don't take no chances with that Clelland."

Lance nodded his head up and down. "Enjoy your breakfast, Jamie."

When he put Clelland's tray under his cell door, Clelland walked up close to the bars.

14

"Good morning, Deputy." He looked down at the tray. "That looks mighty good. Thanks."

Lance was shocked. Clelland was different today. Pleasant. Friendly. Well, that was good.

"Pssst. Pssst," Jamie whispered.

Lance walked back to his cell. "He's setting you up. Don't trust him. Seen animals do the same thing. Nuzzle me. Then when I get behind them, they kick me clear across the blacksmith shop."

"I'll be on guard, Jamie," Lance promised. But inside he felt he ought to give Clelland a fair chance. Maybe he had changed. People did sometimes.

After he had washed the breakfast dishes, Lance told the prisoners he would be back soon.

"Don't forget lunch, Deputy," Clelland said. "You cook so good, you make being in jail OK." Then he laughed.

Lance looked at him. Was he joking? Clelland's face was friendly. "Don't worry. I'll be back in time to fix lunch." Lance walked outside. No doubt about it. Clelland acted like a different man.

The mayor's office was a block away. Lance went in. A large man sat at a desk. "Sit down, young fellow. What can I do for you?"

"I'm Charlotte Nelson's nephew. I'm taking her place until she gets out of the hospital," Lance said.

"Fine woman, son. Did you know she won the arm wrestling championship at the fair last year?"

"Nope. But it doesn't surprise me," Lance grinned. "Aunt Charlotte said I should talk to you about starting a library in Wild Card."

"Good idea. Wild Card used to have a city library. Right up until the Second World War. Then the librarian went off to work in a defense plant. Still have the books. All stored in the firehouse. Of course, you might need a few new ones."

Lance felt good. Maybe he would be able to open a library in Wild Card. Clean air. Work he liked. Close to Aunt Charlotte. "That's great, Mayor. I'll start looking for a building."

"Hold it, son. I just said you had a good idea. I didn't say Wild Card would do it. I have to talk to the city council. Then we have to figure out how much opening a library would cost. Then I have to appoint a committee." The mayor looked over his glasses at Lance. "You know, to study the whole idea."

Suddenly Lance didn't feel so good. "How

long will all that take, Mayor?"

"Well, son, the city council meets on Friday. I'll talk to them then. Of course, being Charlotte's nephew won't hurt you. Folks around here think a great deal of your aunt." He stood up. "Let's say I'll get back to you late Friday afternoon." They shook hands.

Slowly Lance walked back to the jail. He could stay with Aunt Charlotte for a short time. But he needed a job. Otherwise he'd have to go back to the city. Back to all that noise and dirty air. Wild Card needed a library. The city council just had to see that.

CHAPTER 4

CLELLAND
TRIES AGAIN

Lance returned to the jail. He fixed lunch. Clelland was still acting friendly. Again Jamie whispered a warning. "Be careful, son. He'll try to fool you."

Lance picked up Clelland's tray to carry it back to the kitchen. Clelland was brushing his black hat. "Good lunch, Lance," he said. Then he stood in front of the mirror. He looked at himself and smiled.

That afternoon Lance rode his motorcycle out of town. It was a dirt bike. He headed across the prairie toward the hills. His thoughts were on the library. Would the council vote to have a library again? He hoped so. He rode up a hill and down the other side. The breeze felt cool on his face. The air smelled fresh. He drove to the top of another hill. He shut off his motor. What a view! He didn't want to leave Wild Card.

Maybe I could get another job, he thought. Not a librarian. Maybe be a deputy for Aunt Charlotte. He laughed out loud. His laugh echoed through the hills. Imagine. Him a deputy! He didn't even like guns. He wore a helmet instead of a ten-gallon hat. He liked tennis shoes, not boots. He drove a motorcycle, not a police car. And a star, he thought, belonged in the sky, not on his chest. He shook his head. Nope, he just wasn't cut out to be a deputy.

When he returned to the jail, he served the two prisoners their supper trays. Then he went back to the kitchen to eat his own meal. Suddenly he heard a cry, "Help! Help!"

He rushed into the big room. He could barely see. Smoke lay in heavy layers. It filled the room.

"Open the cell, Deputy. Don't let us burn to death," Clelland cried. "Help! Help!"

"Lie on the floor," Lance shouted. "Less smoke there. Be right back."

He ran back to the kitchen to get the ring of keys. How did the fire start? Old wiring? He grabbed the keys from the kitchen table. He dashed back into the big room. The smoke was thick, but Lance didn't see any flames.

"Hang on, men. I'll have you out in a minute."

Lance heard Jamie coughing. He went to his

cell first. "You all right?" he asked.

"Yes. Let me out. I'll get the bellows from the blacksmith shop. That'll clear this smoke out in a jiffy." Lance unlocked the cell door. Jamie started at a run out the front door. Then he skidded to a stop. "Lance, don't let Clelland out. He's in no danger. This smoke was just one of his

"Let me out. I'll get the bellows from the blacksmith shop."

tricks. He's trying to escape."

Lance leaned against the front door. How did Clelland make all that smoke? Did Jamie really know it was a trick? Maybe this time Jamie was wrong. Lance didn't want anything to happen to Clelland.

"Help. Have mercy, Deputy," Clelland called. "I can't stand the heat. I can feel the flames."

Lance tried not to listen.

In a few minutes Jamie was back with his bellows. "Bet Charlotte has a fan somewhere in her apartment. That would help." Jamie squeezed the bellows.

"I'll find the fan, Jamie." Lance ran to the kitchen. Nothing there. He looked in a closet. Great! A fan!

The fan and the bellows quickly cleared the room of smoke. Lance and Jamie sat on the front steps of the jail.

"How did he do it, Jamie?" Lance asked.

Jamie held out a wrapper. "Found six or seven of these on the floor by his cell. It's a 'smokey.' Kids set them off on the 4th of July. They make a lot of smoke. That's all."

"Well, it almost worked. Thanks a lot, Jamie," Lance said.

Jamie stood up. "Forget it, son. Glad to help. I'm a little tuckered. I think I'll hit the hay." Jamie walked into his cell and closed the door.

Lance walked by the cells a little later. Jamie was asleep. Clelland stood by the bars.

"Sorry, Deputy," he said. "I was just having a little fun."

"Oh, go roast a marshmallow, Clelland." Lance closed the door to Aunt Charlotte's apartment.

CHAPTER 5

THE COFFEE BREAK

On Thursday morning Lance unlocked the door of Jamie's cell. "Your time is up, Jamie. You're free to go."

"Best jail time I ever spent, son. You're quite a cook." Jamie walked out into the large room. "Charlotte put my wallet and belt away."

Lance opened the desk drawers, but Jamie's wallet and belt weren't there. Then he remembered. The safe in Aunt Charlotte's room. "Be right back, Jamie. I think I know where Aunt Charlotte put them." He hurried into her room and opened the safe. Some safe, Lance thought. It doesn't even lock any more. Quickly he removed the wallet and belt.

Jamie sat at Aunt Charlotte's desk. "Good. You found them." He stood up and put the belt through his pant loops. Then he stuck the wallet in his back pocket. "Thank's Lance. Say hello to

Charlotte when you talk with her." Jamie walked across to Clelland's cell. "So long, Clelland. Try to be good."

Clelland didn't answer. He tilted his hat over his eyes. The toothpick in his mouth pointed straight out like a gun.

Jamie shook Lance's hand. "I'm just across the street at the blacksmith shop if you need anything." He pointed to Clelland's cell. "Be real careful, son. He's a bad one."

Lance walked Jamie to the door. One down and one to go, he thought. He was glad to have only one prisoner to cook for and to watch. Saturday couldn't come too soon. That was the day the officer from California would pick up Clelland.

Still he'd miss Jamie. Now there were just Clelland and him. Lance took a deep breath. He went back inside the jail. For some reason he hated looking at Clelland. He felt uneasy. As if he didn't have control. But Clelland was locked up, Lance told himself. Nothing's changed.

He passed Clelland's cell on his way to Aunt Charlotte's apartment. Clelland's hands gripped the bars tightly. He smiled at Lance. A chill ran down Lance's back. Clelland's smile reminded him of a dog's snarl.

After lunch Lance wheeled his motorcycle into the jail room. He needed to change the oil and the filter.

"Some wheels you got there, Lance." Clelland said. "I always wanted a motorcycle."

Lance looked up at the sound of his voice. "They're lots of fun. Maybe some day you can get yourself one." He stuck the empty can under the oil drain.

"Say, Lance, if you move your bike close to the cell, I'll reach through the bars and wipe down the spokes. They're kinda greasy."

What's he up to now, Lance wondered. Then he was disgusted with himself. The poor guy must be bored. Even cleaning spokes must be better than doing nothing. The words of Jamie flashed through his mind. "Be careful. He's tricky." But what could Clelland do? He was locked in his cell. No way was Lance going to unlock that door.

"Well? Want my help or not?" Clelland asked.

"Sure. I was just thinking what you'd need to do the job. A clean rag and maybe some ammonia water."

"That should do the trick," Clelland said.

Why did Clelland have to use the word "trick?" I'm getting spooked over nothing, Lance thought. He wheeled the bike up next to the cell. He adjusted the bike stand. Now Clelland could sit on his cell floor and reach through the bars to the spokes. "I'll get you a rag. Aunt Charlotte must have some ammonia in the kitchen. Be right back."

Soon Lance returned with a pan of ammonia water and some clean rags. Clelland sat on his jacket on the cell floor. His black cowboy hat sat on the back of his head.

Soon they both were busy working on the motorcycle. Lance had a screw driver. He was trying to screw the oil pan on.

"Here let me hold the pan. You put the screws in." Clelland reached through the bars and held his hands under the pan.

Finally Lance had the pan back on. "Whew! I always have trouble getting that pan back on. Guess I need another pair of hands. You helped a lot. Thanks."

Now Clelland was standing in front of the mirror again. He took off his hat and combed his hair. Then he set his hat on his head at just the right angle. Again he smiled into the mirror. He turned to Lance. "I was glad to help. You know what would taste good right now? A cup of coffee."

"You're right. A coffee break would hit the spot." Lance headed for the kitchen.

In a few minutes he was back with two cups of hot coffee on a tray. He'd even found some cookies. But, as he walked through the door, he saw Clelland at the door leading outside. He had Aunt Charlotte's gun and holster.

"Stop, Mr. Clelland. I have your coffee." Then he realized how dumb that sounded.

Clelland turned around. "Don't read any books I wouldn't, librarian. See you," he called. He was out the door fast.

Lance set the tray on the floor. He ran to the door. He saw Clelland untie a horse in front of the blacksmith's shop. In a flash he had swung a black boot over the back of the horse and galloped off. A roll of dust followed him.

How did he do it, Lance asked himself. He ran back to the cell. Then he knew. Clelland had picked the cell door lock with Lance's screwdriver! He hadn't wanted coffee. He'd wanted me out of the room, Lance thought. What a jerk I am!

CHAPTER 6

THE PLAN

Lance grabbed his helmet, goggles, and a jacket. He tied a sleeping bag to the back of his motorcycle. On his belt he clipped a canteen of water. Quickly he wheeled his motorcycle out of the jail.

Jamie stood in front of his blacksmith shop. "Took my best mare, the thief." Then he watched Lance climb on the bike. "You aren't going after him, are you?"

"Yes." Lance fixed the rear view mirror. "I've got to. It's my fault he got away."

"How did he get the keys?" Jamie asked.

"Didn't. He opened his cell door with a screw driver. You were right, Jamie. He's a slick one, all right. He conned me but good." Lance felt anger at himself boil inside. Cool down, buddy, he thought. Getting mad won't get you out of this jam. He took a deep breath and held it. He began to feel calmer.

"What you need is a posse." Jamie held on to the handlebars of the motorcycle. "Clelland is heading for the hills. There's no way you can track him alone. Let alone arrest him."

"You might be right, Jamie. But I have to try." Lance put on his goggles. He zipped up his leather jacket.

"Son, those hills have a hundred hiding places. There are valleys and gullies. Caves and cliffs. He could hide out forever up there."

"Not forever, Jamie. He'll need food and water," Lance said.

Jamie stepped back. "All right. If you're set on doing it. I still say a posse is the only way." Then he looked closely at Lance's waist. "Where's your gun."

"I don't carry a gun." Lance didn't tell Jamie that Clelland had taken Aunt Charlotte's gun. He could tell that Jamie already thought he wasn't much of a deputy.

"See you, Jamie." Lance stepped down on the starter pedal. The motor caught. With a wave of his hand Lance roared out of town toward the hills.

In the distance he saw the roll of dust. If he could just catch up with Clelland before he got to the hills, Lance thought. Then he thought again. How could I capture him if I did catch up with him? He has a gun. He's stronger and bigger than I am. Lance felt cold fear in his belly. It spread in shivers up his back. Bigger and stronger, he thought, but not smarter. Somehow I have to outsmart him.

The prairie was rough with gopher holes, rocks, and ditches. Lance didn't slow down. He seemed to be gaining on the cloud of dust ahead of him. Suddenly the dust cleared. There was the horse. Lance looked around. Where was Clelland?

He parked his motorcycle a few feet from where the horse stood. He got off. With slow, easy steps he moved closer to the horse. He knew he should say something to the horse. He was a city boy. How should he know what to say to a horse?

"Nice horsie." Lance held out his hand, palm up. "Whoa. Easy does it." He moved closer. But now the horse backed up. "Whoa. Hey, pal, I'm a friend."

One more step and he'd be close enough to grab the reins. "Nice horseeeee." He reached out. The reins were in his hand. Now what to do? There was no tree to tie the horse to. He led the

30

animal toward the motorcycle. He could tie him to that. Then he could look around the base of the hill. He started toward the bike. Then he knew why Clelland had left the horse. The poor animal was lame. He must have stepped in a gopher hole or something. Slowly he led the horse to the motorcycle. He looped the reins around the handlebars. He looked up towards the hills. Not a sign of Clelland.

A shot rang out. Lance ducked behind his motorcycle. The echo of the shot repeated four times. Bang! Bang! Bang! Bang! The echo slowly faded away. Carefully he looked around his bike. Nothing moved on the hill. He looked at the rock formations. The sound of the shot had bounced off one high rock, then another and another and another. Four times. Very interesting.

Then Lance knew how he could trick Clelland.

CHAPTER 7

TRICKED, TRAPPED, AND WISED-UP

The first thing Lance did was untie the horse. He knotted the reins around the horse's neck. With a sudden clap of his hands he sent the horse running. She wasn't running fast because of her lame leg. She was heading toward town.

Then Lance cupped his hands to his mouth. "Clelland. I'm unarmed."

Clelland stepped out from behind a rock high upon the hill. "I'm not," he shouted. He fired off three shots, one right after another.

Lance ducked behind his bike again. Now, Lance thought, Clelland has only two bullets left. Lance scooted on his belly behind a large rock. When he was some distance from his bike, he called out, "A posse's on the way."

Clelland aimed toward the sound of the voice. He fired the last two bullets in the revolver. Lance sighed with relief. Now they were evenly matched. Neither of them had a gun. Of course, Clelland was still bigger and stronger. But Lance hoped to even that up by using his head!

It was late afternoon. The sun was setting. The side of the hill was in shadow now. Even Lance and his motorcycle were in shadows.

"Hey, Deputy, let's make a deal." Clelland

Clelland stepped out from behind a rock. He fired three shots one after another.

stepped out from behind a rock.

"What sort of deal?"

"I'll take your bike."

"That's no deal, Clelland."

"It's a deal for your life, Deputy. I'll take your bike and," Clelland gave a mean laugh, "not kill you. Now that's what I call a good deal."

"No deal. Posse's on the way."

"There's no posse. You're bluffing," Clelland screamed.

"Believe me. I'm telling it like it is." Lance started gathering twigs and dry brush. He stacked them in a pile.

"Fool! Just wait until it's dark. I'll get you then," Clelland called. He went back behind the rock.

Icy fingers of fear tripped down Lance's spine. His plan had to work! It was a simple one. It was based on Clelland's liking himself so much. Lance remembered how Clelland had smiled at himself in the mirror. He also remembered how Clelland had bragged about being wanted in three states. Lance figured that Clelland would do anything not to be caught by a young, new deputy. But if Clelland thought a huge posse had to be gathered to catch him, he'd be proud. And pride goes before a fall. The trick was to let him think there was a posse.

It was dark now. The moon was beginning to rise. Lance could see his motorcycle gleam in the moonlight. He was sure Clelland could see it, too. It was an easy way to escape. Lance was sure Clelland couldn't resist the bait.

Quietly Lance climbed a small hill just above the motorcycle. He called out, "Got you surrounded, Clelland."

The echo repeated, "Surrounded, Clelland" four times.

"Come on down," Lance called.

"On down," the echo said. "On down, on down, on down."

There was no answer. Lance knew Clelland was still up there and needed the motorcycle to escape. Now Lance was ready for the set-up. Quickly he slid down the side of the hill. He called out, "Sound off, Harry." He dragged out the name, "Har-ry."

The echo repeated "Har-ry" loud and clear. Again and again and again.

Swiftly, Lance dodged around the base of the hill to another side. He called out. "You, too, Thomas."

"Thom-as," the echo said. "Thom-as, Thom-as, Thom-as."

He ran quickly from one place to another. He yelled out different names. He made it sound as if there were many men. And they were all ready at the foot of the hill.

"Give him a chance," Lance called. The echo repeated it as if many men were saying the words. "Wait him out. He's got no food. No water." The echo repeated "no water" several times.

Lance waited behind a large rock. Ten minutes passed. A coyote howled in the distance. Lance shivered in the night air. Something scurried in the brush. It sounded as if it were right behind him. Lance thought of snakes. Were they noisy? Or even worse—Clelland. He heard a loose rock tumble down the hillside. That must be Clelland, he thought.

Quietly Lance moved from the rock to a huge sagebrush. Several times he thought he saw a figure—only to have it change in the moonlight.

Then he saw the shadow of Clelland. This time there was no mistake. The shadow wore a dark cowboy hat. Suddenly Clelland jumped out of the darkness. He ran over to the motorcycle. He was looking for the keys.

Quickly Lance moved behind Clelland. He jabbed the hollow end of his marking pen into

Clelland's back. Clelland started to turn around. Lance pressed the end of the marking pen harder. "Hold it, Clelland. Put your hands behind your back."

"Give me a break, Deputy. I'll make it worth your time. You can tell the posse I knocked you out. Just give me the motorcycle key and I'll leave."

"No tricks this time, Clelland. And there's no screw driver out here." Lance snapped the handcuffs on his wrists.

"The posse will never know. I'll leave the county." Clelland's voice was full of fear now.

"Posse? What posse? There's just me," Lance laughed, "me and the echo."

"You tricked me!" Clelland's face twisted in anger.

"You tricked yourself, Clelland. You were so sure I couldn't bring you in all by myself."

Lance spread his sleeping bag on the ground. He lit the brush and twigs he had gathered earlier. "We'll wait until dawn," he said.

"You mean stay here?" Clelland asked.

"Yes." Lance knew it was too dangerous to ride to town in the dark. The prairie wasn't a paved highway.

"Got anything to read?" Clelland sat down on

the sleeping bag.

"The library is closed and keep your mouth the same way." Lance wasn't going to be conned again.

CHAPTER 8

AUNT CHARLOTTE'S TRICK

The sun rose. It cast a golden glow over the prairie. Lance rolled up the sleeping bag. He tied it on the back of his motorcycle. He stomped out the fire. Then he kicked dirt over it.

"You sit on the sleeping bag, Clelland." Lance helped Clelland climb on the motorcycle.

"Hey, man. You trying to kill me? How can I stay on with my hands cuffed?"

"That's your worry, Clelland. I'll snap your belt to mine with these cords. That'll help you balance. Hug your knees to the side of the bike."

In a few minutes they were heading for Wild Card. Lance tried to ride the smoothest way. He avoided holes and ditches as much as possible. He heard Clelland's mumbling to himself. Halfway there, Lance stopped.

"Want to stretch a moment, Clelland?" he asked.

"Naw. I'll ride it through. I'd like it if you'd stop just before we get to town. I want to comb my hair." He stopped a moment. "Wish it was dark. People don't expect a guy like me to be taken by the likes of you. It's embarrassing."

"I know. You're wanted in three states. I've heard it all before." Lance shook his head. This guy was a real zero.

Lance did stop on the edge of town. Clelland had a hard time combing his hair with his hands cuffed. Lance put the black hat on his head for him. "There. You look good enough for any WANTED poster."

They drew up in front of the jail. A station wagon with a California license was parked in the driveway.

"Must be the officer to take you to California," Lance said. He helped Clelland off the motorcycle. He walked behind him into the jail.

There at the desk sat Aunt Charlotte. "Welcome back, Clelland. How be you, Lance?" She tossed the cell keys to Lance. "Lock him up."

Lance led Clelland to the cell. He locked him in. "Now hold out your wrists. I'll take the handcuffs off."

Aunt Charlotte laughed. "You've learned a lot

since you've been here, Lance."

Lance hurried over to his aunt. He hugged her tight. "Boy, am I glad to have you home." He looked down at her leg. "Can you walk with that cast?"

"You bet I can, Lance. But I won't be roller

"Welcome back, Clelland. How be you, Lance?"

skating for a while. That's why I bought that trampoline. Keep me in shape." She pointed to a small trampoline set up in the corner of the room.

"Right," Lance agreed with a grin. Aunt Charlotte! There was no one quite like her. "What is that station wagon doing out in the driveway? I thought it might be the officer to take Clelland back to California."

"You're right. The guy's visiting his cousin. He'll pick up the prisoner after lunch. Speaking of which, I'd better get cooking." Aunt Charlotte stood up and was halfway to the door before Lance remembered her cast.

"I'll fix lunch, Aunt Charlotte. You rest," he said.

"Nonsense, Lance. You shower and shave. You want to look like a librarian, not some bounty hunter. The mayor is coming over to give you the job of running the library."

"Terrific! Now I'm really glad I came to Wild Card." Lance headed for the shower.

After Lance had cleaned up, he served lunch to Clelland. Clelland took one bite of the pork and beans and shoved the tray back under the door. "That woman's cooking is cruel and unusual punishment."

Lance laughed. It felt good to know he was no longer a deputy. No more worries about looking after the jail. He could hardly wait for the mayor to come. He'd take the job — fast! After all, it meant working in a nice town with clean air doing the work he knew and loved. He would be close to Aunt Charlotte. What more could a guy ask for?

It was just after one o'clock. The mayor greeted Aunt Charlotte warmly. Then he pulled a contract from his inside pocket.

Lance quickly signed his name.

"Now you do realize that you are the librarian of Wild Card. That means you'll have to unpack books, order books, collect fines. You know, do library stuff."

"Right, mayor. I understand." Lance could hardly wait to get started.

"And when your Aunt Charlotte needs a deputy, you're it."

"What?" Lance asked. "Oh, no!"

"Says so right in the contract you signed," the mayor said.

"Don't worry, Lance." Aunt Charlotte bounced up and down on her trampoline. "I'll probably never have to call on you again." She jumped higher. "And it was the only way the council could afford a full-time librarian. You know Wild Card is just a small town."

"All right. I accept—but I should have my head examined," Lance said.

Aunt Charlotte clapped her hands and jumped again. She missed and landed on her back. "Oh! Oh! I can't get up. It's my trick back. It goes out every so often."

The mayor said, "It's all right, Charlotte. Just take it easy." He turned to Lance with a twinkle in his eye. "Well, Deputy, looks like you're on duty again!"